Chris Skinner

CAPTAIN CAKE

Meet the Candy Crew

mc Marshall Cavendish
Children

Chapter One
The Candy Crew
Comes to Life

This is just a plain old cake on a plate.

It sits on the plate with a bar of chocolate,
a mound of jelly and, for some reason, a sweet potato.

Suddenly, a beam of light shines over the plate
and the plain old cake becomes Captain Cake.

The beam of light comes from General Rock's
special ray gun, and everything else
on the plate also comes to life.

General Rock needs a crew
for his new spaceship,
The Sweet Candy.

Captain Cake meets with General Rock and Commander Pickle.

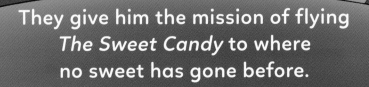

They give him the mission of flying *The Sweet Candy* to where no sweet has gone before.

Captain Cake accepts the mission
and gathers the crew.

General Rock tells them that
they will be known as the Candy Crew.

Before they begin their journey,
they need to learn of their superpowers.

Captain Cake discovers that he can blast cream and jam from his hands.

Lieutenant Chocolate can blast caramel and chocolate chunks from his hands.

Sergeant Jelly can blast jelly from her hands.

Private Potato cannot blast anything from her hands, but she does not want to anyway.

As the pilot of *The Sweet Candy*, Private Potato is an important member of the Candy Crew.

Chapter Two
The First Mission

Captain Cake gets a call from Commander Pickle.

Commander Pickle has run out of apple juice!

He needs the Candy Crew to go to Planet Juice
as soon as possible to get some more.

Captain Cake calls up
the Candy Crew.

Lieutenant Chocolate, who follows his brain and not his heart, turns up.

Sergeant Jelly, who is great at solving tricky problems, turns up.

Private Potato, who has many practical skills, turns up.

The Candy Crew members
have different skills and powers
that work well together.

Lieutenant Chocolate is logical and always works out what to do. He can also blast caramel and chocolate chunks from his hands.

Sergeant Jelly is clever and dependable.
She can blast jelly from her hands.

While Private Potato does not have
a superpower, she can fly spaceships
and fix anything that is broken.

Captain Cake can blast cream and jam from his hands. He is strong and fearless.

Do you know what being fearless means? It means to be brave, but it can also mean acting without thinking.

This is why Captain Cake gets into trouble sometimes.
Do you ever get into trouble?

If you get into trouble,
your friends can help you out.
This is why Captain Cake
needs the rest of the Candy Crew.

Captain Cake tells the Candy Crew their mission.

Private Potato asks where Planet Juice is
so she can plot their way there.

Captain Cake gives her the details
and everyone jumps into their seats.
Private Potato sets the directions to Planet Juice.

"Private Potato, are you ready?" asks Captain Cake.

"Yes, Captain Cake, locked and loaded!" replies Private Potato.

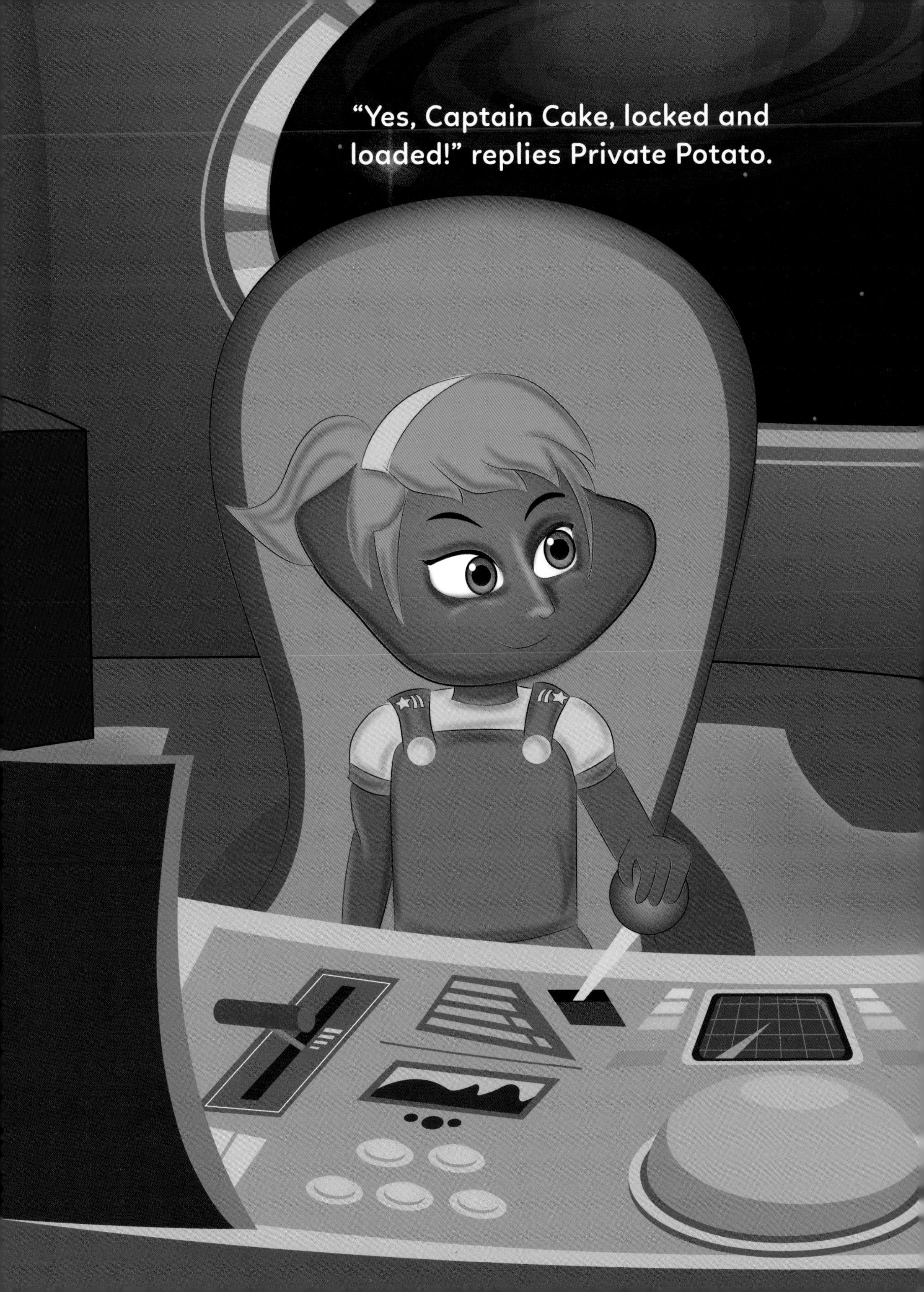

Captain Cake gives
the signal for take-off.

The Candy Crew's adventure begins!

Chapter Three
Lost in Space

Lieutenant Chocolate wakes up and finds himself lost in space. It is dark.

He has no idea where Captain Cake,
Sergeant Jelly and Private Potato might be.

He tries to call them, but no one answers.
He thinks he is on his own.

Lieutenant Chocolate has a superpower, however.
He can blast chocolate chunks and caramel
from his hands. He is made of chocolate
on the outside and caramel on the inside after all!

He is very good at solving tough problems.
He is also good at being logical.

He is in the dark and
he can't find his friends.

What do you think
Lieutenant Chocolate
will do next?

Lieutenant Chocolate looks around.
He finds that it is not completely dark.
He sees a small speck of light in the distance.

He walks towards the speck of light.
As he gets nearer, he sees it growing bigger.

When he reaches the light,
he touches it, but nothing happens.

What would you do if you were him?

Lieutenant Chocolate looks around again and sees that another speck of light has appeared.

He walks towards the second speck of light.
As he gets nearer, he sees it growing bigger.

When he reaches the second light,
he touches it, but nothing happens.

What would you do if you were him?

Thinking logically, Lieutenant Chocolate
looks around again and sees a third speck of light.

Lieutenant Chocolate follows light after light
to try to find his way out of the dark.

This is because Lieutenant Chocolate is very logical.
He works out what to do when things are difficult.

And he is right!

After following many specks of light,
he reaches the final one. When he touches it,
all the lights turn on.

Lieutenant Chocolate is on *The Sweet Candy*
and the crew members are all asleep.
He is not lost in space after all!

Using logic, Lieutenant Chocolate found the light switch in the dark.

Unfortunately, the other crew members are now awake! They are upset at being woken up in the middle of the night.

Lieutenant Chocolate tells them that he is sorry and goes to turn off the lights.

Now he has to make his way to his bed in the dark. Fortunately, he remembers the path he needs to take.

Lieutenant Chocolate is logical.
He uses logic to decide what to do.
Whenever the Candy Crew
has a problem, he will solve it
by thinking and acting logically.

Can you be logical?

Lieutenant Chocolate falls asleep
as *The Sweet Candy* continues its flight
to Planet Juice, sweetly going where
no sweet has gone before.

Chapter Four
Sergeant Jelly Saves Captain Cake

The Sweet Candy touches down on Planet Juice.

Sergeant Jelly is looking forward to exploring the planet with the Candy Crew.

They are on Planet Juice to get
apple juice for Commander Pickle.
He finished all of the apple juice on his ship.

The lakes, rivers and seas on Planet Juice
are filled with juice. There are many flavours of juice,
including orange, pineapple and cranberry.

The *Sweet Candy* lands next to the Beetroot Sea.

Captain Cake,
Lieutenant Chocolate
and Sergeant Jelly
alight from the spaceship.

Suddenly, Captain Cake
slips and falls into
the Beetroot Sea.

Oh no! Captain Cake does not know how to swim!

"No problem," says Sergeant Jelly.
She knows how to swim.

She changes into her jelly form
and jumps into the sea.

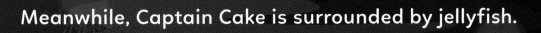
Meanwhile, Captain Cake is surrounded by jellyfish.

Sergeant Jelly swims under Captain Cake
and pushes him towards the surface.

Lieutenant Chocolate mistakes
Sergeant Jelly for a jellyfish.

Can you tell the difference
between jelly and jellyfish?

Lieutenant Chocolate gets ready
to blast chocolate and caramel
at Sergeant Jelly.

"NO!" Captain Cake cries.
"It's Sergeant Jelly!"

"STOP!" Sergeant Jelly shouts.
"It's me!"

Lieutenant Chocolate stops his chocolate and caramel blast just in time.

He helps Captain Cake and Sergeant Jelly out of the red water.

Phew! Captain Cake thanks Sergeant Jelly
for saving him from the jellyfish and the Beetroot Sea.

This is what Sergeant Jelly always does.
She bravely rescues the Candy Crew
whenever they are in trouble.

Do you know what being brave means?
It means helping your friends
when they are in trouble.

Sergeant Jelly is the best at this
because she always puts her friends first.

Although it is good to be brave,
we need to think carefully before we act.
Do you think Sergeant Jelly thought carefully
about how to help Captain Cake before
she jumped into the Beetroot Sea?

"Now that we are all safe, let's get that juice
for Commander Pickle," says Lieutenant Chocolate.

They dip jugs into the Apple River
and fill them up with apple juice.

The Candy Crew returns to their spaceship
with a new supply of apple juice
for Commander Pickle

Chapter Five

Private Potato Avoids a Rock Shower

Commander Pickle's spaceship
has broken down. He needs
the Candy Crew to fly
to Planet Gobstopper
on his behalf.

The Candy Crew rushes to
The Sweet Candy and buckle up.

As they head towards
Planet Gobstopper, they come across
a shower of rock candy.

Private Potato needs to avoid the rocks
as they could destroy the spaceship.
She says that it is just like how chomping
on hard candy can spoil your teeth.

She carefully flies the ship around the rocks.
She turns left and right and goes up and down
to avoid crashing into them.

Private Potato has done it!
The Sweet Candy is safe from the rock shower!

Private Potato can fly a spaceship well.
She is a very important member
of the Candy Crew.

She keeps the Candy Crew safe
by flying to places without getting into trouble.

Do you know what being safe means?

It means looking after yourself and your friends so that you do not get into trouble or hurt yourself.

Although Private Potato does not have any superpowers, she is handy.

Do you know what being handy means?

It means being good at doing things
with your hands and being able to fix things.

Private Potato can fix
the spaceship whenever
it needs fixing.

If you give Private Potato something that is broken, she can make it work again.

Do you know how to fix things?

Private Potato is the only crew member
who knows how to fix a spaceship.

Without her, the Candy Crew
would not be able to fly anywhere.

Private Potato and Sergeant Jelly are important members of the Candy Crew.

Private Potato keeps the crew away from trouble,
but if they should get into trouble,
Sergeant Jelly will come to the rescue.

And so the adventure continues...

Captain Cake is the leader of the Candy Crew. He is known as Victor to his friends because he can turn into a Victoria sponge cake and blast cream and jam at bad guys. He is fearless, but because of this, he sometimes gets into trouble as he does not always think carefully before he acts.

Lieutenant Chocolate is very logical and this makes him good at solving problems. He thinks a lot before he acts. He is known to his friends as Karma because he can blast chunks of caramel and chocolate from his hands.

Sergeant Jelly is brave, and she often saves her friends, especially Captain Cake, from trouble. She can turn into jelly and blast jelly at bad guys. She is known as Wobbly to her friends because she wobbles a lot.

Private Potato is the only one who can fix and fly *The Sweet Candy*, the spaceship of the Candy Crew. She is known as Sweetie to her friends because she is the sweetest sweet potato.

Captain Cake is inspired by my sons, Eddie and Freddie,
who I love and thank for this creation.

~ C.S.

© Marshall Cavendish International (Asia) Pte Ltd
Text and illustrations © 2021 Chris Skinner

Published by Marshall Cavendish Children
An imprint of Marshall Cavendish International

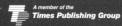
A member of the
Times Publishing Group

Other Marshall Cavendish Offices:
Marshall Cavendish Corporation, 800 Westchester Ave, Suite N-641, Rye Brook, NY 10573,
USA • Marshall Cavendish International (Thailand) Co Ltd, 253 Asoke, 16th Floor, Sukhumvit
21 Road, Klongtoey Nua, Wattana, Bangkok 10110, Thailand • Marshall Cavendish (Malaysia)
Sdn Bhd, Times Subang, Lot 46, Subang Hi-Tech Industrial Park, Batu Tiga, 40000 Shah
Alam, Selangor Darul Ehsan, Malaysia

Marshall Cavendish is a registered trademark of Times Publishing Limited

National Library Board, Singapore Cataloguing in Publication Data

Name(s): Skinner, Chris, author, illustrator.
Title: Meet the Candy Crew / Chris Skinner.
Description: Singapore : Marshall Cavendish Children, 2021.
Identifier(s): OCN 1227472471 | ISBN 978-981-49-2863-2 (paperback)
Subject(s): LCSH: Human-alien encounters--Juvenile fiction. | Friendship--Juvenile fiction. |
Courage--Juvenile fiction.
Classification: DDC 428.6--dc23

Printed in Singapore